The Deception

Gloria Graham

Gotham Books
30 N Gould St.
Ste. 20820, Sheridan, WY 82801
https://gothambooksinc.com/

Phone: 1 (307) 464-7800

© 2022 Gloria Graham. All rights reserved.

No part of this book may be reproduced, stored in a retrieval system, or transmitted by any means without the written permission of the author.

Published by Gotham Books (October 20, 2022)

ISBN: 979-8-88775-112-2 (sc)
ISBN: 979-8-88775-113-9 (e)

Because of the dynamic nature of the Internet, any web addresses or links contained in this book may have changed since publication and may no longer be valid.

The views expressed in this work are solely those of the author and do not necessarily reflect the views of the publisher, and the publisher hereby disclaims any responsibility for them.

Scene 1

Woman and her husband are giving their daughter a bath. They are laughing because the little girl is splashing the bubbles at her parents. While bathing the little girl the wife starts to drift off in thought (Wife starts having memories that frightens her and has the wife asking questioning, now looking puzzled at what was happening in the bathroom) Wife stops washing her daughter. Wife with a fear and panic on her face starts questioning her husband.

Margaret: *"Jason why are we washing this little girl?"* (Margaret staring at the child as if she did not know who the child in the bath tub was?"

Jason: *"Margret Honey what is wrong? This is your daughter Mira you are acting like you don't know your own daughter."*

Margaret: *"This is not my child what is this child doing in my house and why am I washing her?"*

The woman starts to drift off almost into a sleep state. As the mother drifts off. The child looks at the father and speaks.

(Child **Mira**): *"It doesn't seem like it is working."*

(Father **Jason**): *"Please let's not tell anyone, just give it a little more time. She has a good days and bad days but it is working."*

Mother seems to come out of her slumber.

    Margaret: *"I must have drifted off a for a little bit".* Daughter and Father start to laugh.

    Jason: *"Just for a few seconds, you need to get more rest."*

    Margaret: *"You are right work has been really stressful."*

    Jason: *"You did not miss much Mira is all done."*

    Margaret: *"okay my darling little girl time to put on your pajamas and get to bed. I will read you a bedtime story."*

Scene 2

The next day the father is at his office at the Marketing Company. Jason is sitting at his desk leaning back on his chair with his hands behind his head. He suddenly moves forward and unlocks the side draw. He pulls out a picture that he has hidden in his desk. It is a picture of a young woman in her late 20teens. The woman with a small built, long brown hair and a warm loving smile. Jason stares at the picture and becoming tearful while looking at the girl in the picture. The door opens, Jason hurries and puts the picture back in the draw and wipes his eyes.

Secretary Mary: "Jason are you alright?"

Jason: "yes, this weather has my sinuses going crazy."

Mary: "I have been feeling that way for a few days, one minute it is raining and cold then sunshine. Well Jason you have someone here to see you a Mr. Steward should I let him in?"

Mr. Steward comes in the room and Jason quickly stands up.

Jason: "Yes, please…. let."

Before Jason could finish his sentence, Mr. STEWART was standing in the office.

Jason: "Thank you Mary."

(Mary leaves and closes the door).

Jason: "I did not expect you here it has been less than a month since the last time."

Steward:" I know you think you can keep things from me but I heard that Margret was having some memory issues."
Jason:" It was no big deal she was able to come back. We need to give her some time. Work has been stressing her out. If it was something I thought was too much I would notify all of you." Please let me handle it Please."

Steward: "If this becomes an issue, we will handle ourselves." Stewart hands Jason I wooden box with strange carving on top of it. "Stewart, *you know what to do with this."* Jason nods his head with a sad look on his face.

Jason: "Steward, I said it wasn't an issue I promise you that it won't be an issue. She is coming along just fine sometimes she has flashbacks I reassure Her that they are just false memories."

Stewart: "Have you shown her the pictures of her pregnancy? All the things that we gave you so she could see that Mira *is her child."*

Jason:" Yes, she has all the pictures and we go over them together."

Stewart: "Good I will be checking in on you to make sure that everything is going just fine".

Steward gives Jason a piercing look before leaving the office.

Scene 3

Margaret arrives at the school to pick up Mira. Margaret asked Miss. Bishop, Mira's teacher if she could talk to her for a moment outside the classroom.

Margaret: *"Does Mira seem different from the other students?*

Miss. Bishop looks over at Margaret with a strange look on her face.

Miss. Bishop: *"what do you mean by different?"*

Margaret: *"I mean does she seem a little different from the other kids? I mean does she act different or is there something that you noticed that is different from the other children?"*

Miss. Bishop: *"No miss Campbell she is an excellent student actually Mira is well advanced in class more advanced than her peers. I was really thinking about asking you and your husband if we could maybe advance Mira to a higher grade because she's doing the work of a second grader and she's only in the kindergarten. I just don't want her to get bored because she seems to be a little bored with some of the things she's learning in class because she moves faster and finishes a lot sooner than her peers."* looks at Margaret with a questionable stare and says "*was there something that you noticed that you want to talk about?"*

Margaret: *"No, I was just checking to see if there was anything we should be aware of. Well thank you for your time".*

Mira come running out of the class room putting her arms around her mother's waist.

Margaret: *"time to go home". With a smile.*

MIRA: *"Bye Miss Bishop see you on Monday."*

Mira leaves with her mother holding hands Mira turns her head slightly in the direction of Miss Bishop making eye contact and gives Miss Bishop a darting stare as Miss Bishop looks at Mira and nods.

Scene 4

Jason is lying beside Margaret who is fast asleep. Jason looks over with tears in his eyes before getting out of bed. Jason slowly walks down the stairs into the garage where the box that steward had given him. He slowly pulls it out of the trunk of his car. Closing the trunks softly and walks back up the stairs and opens his bedroom door where his wife is sound asleep, he hesitates to open the box but he remembers that Stewart told him. Jason slowly opens the box and inside the wooden box wrapped in a green satin cloth is a crystal that begins to laminated.

Jason hesitates though he knows what must be done, what he has to do to keep his family safe and to help Margaret. He places small round crystal on Margaret's back. As Jason places the crystal it takes on unknown forms. Margaret starts to move just slightly. Jason is careful and watches that she does not awaken. After a few minutes Jason takes the crystal off Margaret's back with tears in his eyes and places it back into the wooden box as he slowly closes the bedroom door and walks back down the stairs to the garage placing the wooden box back into the trunk. Jason sits on the couch before he goes back up the stairs shaking his head as he looks at the pictures of his wife and his daughter. Jason knows what he had no choice as he goes back upstairs. First checking his daughter's room. Mira is she sound asleep and now he walks back in his room and slowly climbs into the bed and covers himself before he falls asleep, he looks at Margaret one more time.

Scene 5

It the weekend and Margaret and Mira up early making breakfast with the whole house smelling like pancakes, eggs and sausage. Both Margaret and Mira are laughing and talking about the silliest things. Jason enters the kitchen with a smile and says "what are you girls doing?"

Mira: *"Me and mom are making breakfast for us and you too dad. Mom was telling me the silly story about the beach and how I covered you up with sand and it was so much fun. Mom also told me the day I was born and how fat my cheeks were and she thought she would never be able to push me out because my cheeks were so fat."*

After Jason had heard what Mira had said he felt so relieved he knew that what he did Last night was worth it his wife's memory was back. Jason would be able to call Stewart now and let him know that he had nothing to worry about that Margaret remembers. Jason Margaret and Mira finished their breakfast and they decided since it was such a nice day they would go to the park. Mira played as Jason and Margaret talked about things from the past and all the happy memories.

Scene 6

Margaret:" Good morning, Mira good morning, Jason. Jason, do you think you could take Mira to school today? I have a slight headache so I'm just going to go straight to work and see how much I can finish today I have two clients coming in this morning to look at some prints and then I think I'm just going to come home and lie down for a little bit."

Jason:" Hey Hun is there anything I can do for you. I have something for a headache if you need it."

Margaret: "No it's not that bad just a little slight headache but I'll be fine."

Jason:" Well, all right little lady let's go time for school. Margaret arrives at work her secretary Aisha greets her with a smile."

Margaret: " that would be great Aisha I think I have this headache because I didn't have any coffee all weekend."
Both women laugh and Aisha leaves to pick get the coffee for Margaret.
Margaret drinking her coffee staring into space as someone knocks on the door. It is Aisha with her last client to look at some swatches.

Margaret:" Aisha I have no more clients today so I'm going to go home and get some rest if I have any calls, please just take my messages and I'll return them tomorrow." **Aisha:** "We'll do Mrs. Campbell get some rest. See you tomorrow."

Margaret arrives at home gets comfortable and lies down in bed. She falls asleep Immediately.

Margaret begins to toss and turn as she dreams about a little boy and in her dream, she's playing and laughing in the pool.

Margaret jumps out of her sleep, sweating looking around the room wondering who was this little boy in her dream it felt so real.

Jason and Mira arrive home And Margaret is making dinner.

    Jason: "how's your headache honey is it all gone? Are you feeling better?"

Margaret doesn't want to tell Jason about the dream because she feels he already thinks she's crazy so she keeps the dream from him.

    Margaret: "Yes, all I needed was my morning coffee and an afternoon rest now I feel great."

Margaret smiles at Jason but still refuses to tell Jason about the dream of the little boy.

Scene 7

Margaret: "Jason I seen some girls from my old college days. They are planning a little reunion just 5 or 6 of my close's college friends. We lost touch after college but I found one of them on the school alumni site. I was thinking it might be fun to get away. They are getting together in Cancun. I could go for a vacation do you think it'd be alright"?

Jason: "You know that sounds like fun. Go ahead. When do you plan on leaving?"

Margaret: "They were planning it two weeks from today. I'm kind of excited. It has been 20 years since I hung out with that group from college."

Jason starts to ponder in his head what happens if she's on the vacation and her memory starts coming back. Jason decides to call Stewart to see if there's something that could be done to ensure that Margaret memories do not return while she is on vacation.

Jason: "Margaret, I think it would be best if you speak with your doctor and make sure that he has something to help you with those headaches. I notice that you've been having them a lot lately so go see the doctor before you go on vacation to see what he can give you just in case the headaches come back."

Margaret: "Jason do you really think it's necessary I mean they're not really bad headaches but yeah, I agree with you maybe I should just talk to the doctor before I leave because I really want to have a good time and I don't want any issues on my vacation in Cancun. (Margaret with a big smile on her face). I don't want anything to interfere with our get together."

Margaret says with a big smile.

Margaret makes an appointment at doctor McCall's office.

Margaret schedules an appointment for the next day to speak with the doctor. To see if something she can do about the headaches.

The next day Margaret enters into Dr. McCall's office secretary says good morning.

Margaret: "Good morning I have an appointment with doctor McCall at 9:15."

Secretary: "yes, have a seat miss Campbell and the doctor will be right with you. He is with another patient he should be finished in just a moment."

Margaret sits down and picks up a magazine and starts reading. Doctor McCall comes out of his office.

Stewart: "Hi Margaret."

Margaret: "Hi doctor McCall".

Stewart: "Margaret, we have known each other for a while now you can just call me Stewart."

Margaret: "OK Stewart."

Stewart in Margaret walking to office and close the door he shuts the door behind him.

Stewart: "So, what brings you into the office today?"

Margaret:" Sometimes I have these headaches they're really not that bad, but Jason suggested that I would speak with you because I plan on going on a vacation with some of my girls from college and I just don't want to have a headache and mess up the vacation. It's been a while since I see my friends from college".

Stewart:" I can understand Jason's concern but it's fine I have something that's definitely going to help those headaches." Stewart gets up from his desk and walks over to a cabinet and pulls out a bottle of pills."

Stewart:" So just take one every day and it was going to help with those headaches so that way you could have a wonderful vacation. I can I can see that you are very stressed and this seems like a well needed vacation. So don't forget to take them every day and this will stop those headaches but you have to take them every day. Don't worry there's no side effects with this medication. If you like you can have a few drinks with your friends but don't over, do it. The medication is not going to interfere with you fun. So just have some fun enjoy yourself. If you need anything else don't hesitate to call."

Stewart with a smile on his face stands up from the chair and walks Margaret to the door.

Margaret: "Thanks doctor McCall oh sorry I mean Stewart."

Margaret smiles and Stewart smiles back at her as she walks away. Margaret gets into her car and drives away.

Jason walks in from a hidden door in the back of Stewart's office where he has been hiding throughout Stewart's and Margaret's visit. Listening to the conversation.

Stewart walks back into the office seeing Jason closes the door behind him.

Jason:" Stewart how does she seem to you?'

Stewart:" You're right Jason the treatments are working. As long as you keep it up. Margaret must remember to take that medication I have given her while vacation. Everything should be fine. All her past memories will be gone and the memories that we've implanted will now be permanent memories."

Jason:" Don't worry Stewart I'll make sure That she does what she needs to do. I love my wife and I don't want anything to happen to her. "

Stewart:" Jason you should have thought about that how much you loved your wife before you caused these problems. Not as up to us to make sure that would happen stays quiet and nobody knows. Especially not Margaret and if she does, we'll have to take care of her."

Jason stands up walks through the door slams it behind himself.

Scene 8

Margaret arrives In Cancun and as she goes to the front desk some of her friends call out her name Margaret is that you her friends calling from the other side of the hotel lobby. The first person to run up to her was Candace one of her college friends.

Candace:" girl you haven't changed a bit you still look like you did when you were in college."

Margaret: Margaret says with a smile." I've aged girls you're just being kind."

Candace:" Letisha, Cynthia, Toni come on over here you'll never believe who's standing over here it's Margaret Fleming."

Margaret smiles:" Well, I got married a few years after college so my name is no longer Fleming It's Mrs. Campbell."

Letisha: "Well excuse us Mrs. Campbell. All the women start to laugh."

Cynthia: "We ll ladies let's go up to our Penthouse suite and get Freshened up and come downstairs for a couple drinks." The women are down at the pool having a few drinks and laughing about they're crazy time in college. It has been a long time since they've even talk to each and have no ideal about each other's life after college.

Scene 9

The girls are now downstairs in the lobby waiting for the tour bus to pick them up to take them on the excursion to see the ruins. Margaret remembers that she forgot her sunglasses.

Margaret:" Hey ladies I'll be right back I have to run upstairs and grab my sunglasses I'll just be a minute. "

The girls nod as Margaret runs towards the elevator. As Margaret is walking to her room. I strange woman looks at her as if she knew her.

Margaret Looks at the woman and smiles and nods her head as they say hello. The woman stops Margaret in the hallway before Margaret was able to reach her room.

The Stranger:" Hi I know you probably don't Remember Me my name is Donna Miller and I know it's been a long time but I swear I seen you in New York about several years ago. You were walking with a little boy you were holding his hand and he dropped his action figure. I picked it up and I caught up with you and the little boy. I said I believe this is your son's action figure he dropped it on the sidewalk. Both you and your son thanked me and you told me that that was his favorite toy and you appreciate me picking it up and bringing it back to him. You had on this beautiful wedding ring that was blue sapphire shaped like a teardrop with small diamonds around it. I remember you said that your husband had it specially designed for you and sapphires was your favorite stone but he had to embellish it with those beautiful diamonds all around it."

Donna looks down at Margaret's hand and she's wearing the exact same ring Donna remembers when she met her in New York.

Donna: "That's the ring, I'll never forget it was absolutely beautiful you're wearing it right now so you have to be the person that I met in New York."

Margaret:" Sorry you must be mistaken because I don't have a son. Maybe somebody else has a ring like mine. I have a daughter and she's in kindergarten so maybe you confuse me with someone else."

Donna:" I never forget a face and your son was so cute. Plus, that beautiful ring. I could never forget that ring."

Margaret:" Like I said a don't have a son you are mistaken. Maybe I have a doppelganger because surely wasn't me. Well, it was really nice talking to you but I'm in a hurry my friends are waiting for me downstairs in the lobby we're on our way to see the ruins so you have a nice day and take care."

Donna has this strange look on her face shrugs her shoulders and walks away.

Donna starts to replay the event in her mind she can remember everything that happened that day and becomes very confused why this woman is denying having a son and seeing her and speaking with her in New York.

The women are now back from their Excursion and hot and sweaty so they decided to go upstairs to the suite get freshened up and meet in a few hours meet for dinner.

When Margaret arrives to her room, she starts to feel a headache coming on and decides to take a quick catnap. Margaret decides not to take the pills that that Stewart gave her but just to lie down and see if the headache will go away. Margaret falls fast asleep while she's sleeping, she again dreams about the little boy. She can see the action figure in his hand.

Margaret jumps out of her sleep goes into the bathroom and washes her face as she's looking at herself in the mirror, she tells herself that it's it was just a dream. I don't have a little boy that Donna has no idea what she's talking about.

Scene 10

The next day Margaret was going to have breakfast with her friends. But before walking into the dining room Margaret stopped at the front desk.

Margaret:" *Maybe you can help me I'm looking for a guest I believe her name is Donna Miller. I was wondering what room she was in we were talking yesterday and I forgot to ask her room number.*"

The woman at the Front desk had a shiny name tag that read Terra.

Terra:" *Sorry ma'am but we don't have a guest by that name you did say Donna Miller correct.*"

Margaret:" *Yes, that's what she said Donna Miller and she's a guest at this hotel.*"

Terra:" *Sorry ma'am like I said there's no guests by that name. Are you really sure that was her name because there's no one registered by that name sorry? Have a nice day.*"

Margaret is now frustrated and confused. She could feel herself having a headache so before going to the dining room to meet the girls for breakfast she goes back up to her room to get that medicine that Dr. Stewart told her would help her headaches.
After Margaret leaves the front desk, the camera moves to the backroom where the staff keeps their personal belongings. On the floor are wet footprints.

The film recalls what happened while Donna was taking a morning swim.

Early that morning Donna is out in the ocean alone having a morning swim. Donna is swimming and then all of a sudden you see her being yanked down into the water she's fighting to get back to surface but she's pulled down into the water. All you can see are bubbles on the surface of the water.

Scene 11

The women are at the airport and going their separate ways. They are hugging outside the airport. Each woman lives in a different states and Cynthia lives in Paris France, Letisha Pittsburgh and Toni lives in Chicago.

The women say their good byes and rush off to find the departure gate.

Margaret is smiling as she thinks about all the fun her and the other women had on their get away. As she is laying down in first class that memory of Donna resurfaces. First Margaret ponders over what Donna said about New York and a son.

Margaret shakes head and says to herself "there is no way." She giggles and takes 2 of the pills that Stewart gave her for headaches and a sleeping medication to relax. Margaret was to be rested and in a good when Jason and Mira meet her at the airport.

Margaret's is thinking to herself, nonstop flight from Cancun to Seattle – Tacoma International Airport will give me 6 ½ hours to sleep. Margaret remembers that the airport is about 2.5 miles near Olympic. Margaret now sleeping with her earphones listening to ocean waves is now asleep with no dreams of the little boy.

Scene 12

Margaret:" Good morning, Mira."

Mira: "Mom when did you get home, I miss you so much."

Margaret:" I came home last night I took a shuttle home but I didn't want to wake you, you were sleeping so peacefully. But today I have a surprise for you. You're going to stay home with me I called your teacher and I told her you would not be in today. So, I could spend some time with you. Whatever you want to do today just the two of us. Daddy's Left for work already work. So, it's just going to be you and me baby girl."

Both Margaret and Mira laughed and hugged each other. Jason after work drives down to the compound to meet with some of the elders.

Jason decides to pull over at the abandoned gas station. The same gas station that he used to stop at and talk to the old gas station attendant. Bill was a very old man who ran the gas station by himself because he did not have any family. Jason sits and starts for reminisce about the beginning the first time he met Caroline.

Jason Relives in his mind the events that happened years ago. Jason drives up to the gas station to fill up his tank and bill comes out.

Bill:" Hi Sir how may I help you today? Do you need a fill up and would you like me to check your oil? "

Jason:" Hi yes fill it up and it would be great if you could check my oil. I heard out this way there is a beautiful lake and I *just feel like sitting and looking at the water today just to my mind it's been such a long day. "*

Bill:" I can understand that and it's such a beautiful day to be able to sit back and clear your mind. About 20 miles down the road there is a compound they don't allow anybody in they're pretty cool they're pretty quiet they keep to themselves. But they have a beautiful property I don't know if you can get in. But if you get opportunity there's a Big Lake with a waterfall. I remember as a kid That was before they moved in. Now it's private property. Don't get me wrong they're pretty good folks they come by here every morning to get gas on their way into the city."

Jason:" You said it's about 20 miles down the road? "

Bill:" About 20 miles and then you'll see a sign to the left that says lake you can only go so far before it starts getting gated off but you can try."

Jason:" Well, *wish me luck."*

Bill waves goodbye and Jason drives away heading towards the lake that bill told him about. Jason makes the left and he notices that it is gated that he cannot get in so he pulls his car over to the side. There's he sees a small opening in the wooden gate. He says to himself I wonder if I can make it through that gate. So, Jason wiggles his way through the gate walks down the path and as he's it's closer he can see this beautiful lake with his wonderful waterfall. He walks over to the lake takes his shoes off and never noticing that there's a girl a few yards away from him with her feet dangling in the water. The Girl is looking over at Jason slightly puzzled not knowing who he was or how he got in through the gate.

Tina:" Hello. With a very friendly and sweet voice. Do you know this is private property? I really don't think you're allowed to be here."

Jason:" I'm sorry I didn't mean to interrupted or violate any rules. I know that's private property but I just wanted to go somewhere where I can just clear my mind and I was told that there was a beautiful lake 20 miles down from the gas station gas. The gas station attendant told me all about it. He did say that it was private but I thought maybe I could find my way in."

Tina smiles at Jason and it was the sweetest smile that Jason has seen all day.

Tina and Jason introduce themselves. Jason walks closer to where Tina was sitting. Jason made sure that he kept his distance. So, not to make Tina feel uncomfortable. He had already intruded by coming onto the private property. So, the last thing he wanted to do was make her feel uncomfortable. And besides he was enjoying the beautiful view of the lake in the warm breeze in his face. So, he didn't want it give Tina a reason to make him leave.

The two sat there talking and laughing and became very comfortable with each other. Jason and Tina never notice the time. It was getting pretty late the sun was going down.

Tina:" I really had a great time talking to you I never get to talk to anybody outside the compound. So, it was nice to talk to someone other than my family and friends and my neighbors. I hope we could be friends. Maybe you can bring your wife and your son. But they'll have to sneak in too. (With a sweet laugh and smile). This is always a really good time though to come if you want. Everyone in the compound is doing something they're always busy. There is a certain time every day that everyone in the compound comes down to the lake at the same time. I come down to the lake as much as possible it gives me a sense of peace."

Jason:" Well, my wife and my son are not much for the woods they are not lake people either. My son has really bad allergies and my wife doesn't like bugs."

Both Jason and Tina laugh and they say goodbye. Jason walks back to the opening in the gate and climbs into his car. Heads back to the city.

As he is driving back, he's innocently thinking about Tina and how much fun you had today.

Jason arrives home and is greeted by Margaret and Justin his son.

Justin kisses Margaret and kisses his son Justin on the top of his head all three of them sit down for dinner.

For months when Jason feels he needs to get away he finds himself back at the lake. Enjoying more and more time with

Tina. Tina and Jason's few encounters were very innocent. But before they knew it, they become intimate. First it started with and innocent kiss on the cheek just say goodbye. After visiting the lake several times. Before they realized it, they found themselves in each other's arms. Passionate kissing that led to uncontrollable sex. As the two are making love. Jason turns his head to the right and Tina has her head to the left. Both have their eyes closed because they are engaged while entangled in each other's bodies. Because Jason's eyes are closed, he doesn't Tina's face is no longer human. Tina's face has transformed into her true self which is alien.

When Jason had opened his eyes Tina's face had turned back to human into that beautiful young woman that Jason Has fallen in love with.

Scene 13

Jason has now come back to the present and finds himself sitting at the abandoned gas station. He is on his way to the compound to talk to the Elders.

The large gates open and Jason enters into the compound.

Jason enters into the room that resembles a courtroom.

    Jason:" Everything is going as planned. Margaret believes that Mira Is her daughter so can we hurry up and move on with the last phase of this plan? "

Aaron whose true name is Orpha slowly walks over to Jason. As his face starts to transform into the creature that he is. Orpha's arm starts to stretches out from his chest. It looks more like an octopus as this creature grabs Jason by the throat.

    Orpha:" You have the audacity to tell us to hurry up and move on. Remember Jason you came into our compound and you not just trespassed. You violated our code to never mix are people with your people. You had sex with one of ours and created this crossbreed. You not just created an abomination child with one of our people, but you are the cause of Tina's death She was unable to live through the birth of your child. Tina violated the code so her death was punishment and a warning to others not to try it. My people and your people which was told by the elders.

Before we ever decided to come to Is planted, we were safe to know that that could never happen. That it was impossible to reproduce a species crossbreeding with your kind in my kind. We prohibited the interacting of our kind with your humankind. We live amongst you but we don't allow relationships romantic, physical relationships with humans. Now we have to fix your mess so I'd be very careful making demands."

Orpha releases Jason's neck and Orpha' s octopus like arm retracts back into his chest.

Jason turns towards the council as he's rubbing his neck.

Jason:" *May I please see my son? "*

One of the council members stretches out his arms and points towards the door. He is escorted by another council member who opens up two large doors. They enter into this dark room and in the middle of the room is it glass coffin like structure. In this strange structure is a young boy who is connected to multiple probes and seems to be sound asleep.

Jason:" *How long does he have to stay like this? "*

Elder:" Until *everything is complete. He is not in any danger he is fine he's going through the reprogramming process also. Once this is complete and your wives now believes that Mira is her daughter. We will reinstall the memories of your son back to her. Also placing Mira into your son's memory as being the loving big brother. Your wife and your son's will have new memories of all four of you being one big happy family. We are setting up your new location when Margaret and Justin awake. They will be in a new location Margaret will be transferring with you and the children to Colorado. Margaret will tell the company she is leasing the office space. She will no longer need the space because she is moving to Colorado with her husband and family.*

Jason you will tell your firm that you decided to go into business on your own. So, there will be no questions why you are leaving Washington. We have also set up Mira and Justin in to one of our private schools in Colorado. There won't be any questions or any concerns with their transfer. All the children' records including all medical records will be transferred to the private school. We will have people watching to make sure that everything is still going smoothly. We have an office for Margaret for her interior decorating business. You We'll tell your firm that you decided you've decided to open up your own firm marketing firm."

Several weeks later Margaret, Jason Justin, Mira Are now living in Colorado. Justin and Mira are in the family room playing a board game. Margaret and Jason are in the kitchen preparing dinner. Margaret and Justin only remember the four of them as a family.

As Margaret looks into the room at the children laughing and playing.

Margaret:" *Jason aren't we blessed to have two beautiful children and I love Colorado."*

Jason:" *Yes, I feel so blessed to have my beautiful children and my beautiful wife life is great."*

Margaret and Jason embrace and kiss.

As Jason and Margaret are enjoying their family.
 The camera goes back to the compound where a young man is leaping over the fence.

He seems to have some type of strength to be able to clear such a high fence. The fence had long been repaired to prevent unwanted visitors. The elders reinforce the gates and security cameras to prevent what happened with Tina and Jason so to never happen again.

The young man rushes to the car that is running in part on the opposite side of the gate. He gets into the driver side and as he pulls away quickly, he looks over at a young girl that's sitting in the passenger side of the car. They both look frightened but they young man stretches his hand over. He smiles at the female her stomach.

The young man:" Don't *worry babe everything is going to be just fine they'll never find us in Vegas. Vegas here we come."*

They both smile and speed down the highway.

Meanwhile back at the compound the security cameras have caught everything. The security guard watching the camera jumps out of his seat. Runs into the council room to tell what he has seen.

Three of the councilmen Stewart, Orpha, Brackus they use mental telepathy to talk to security guards.

You see 6 men standing at the edge of the lake as they're walking toward the lake they start to transform. They are no longer in their human form; they are now in alien form. Sea creature and they vanish into the water.

www.ingramcontent.com/pod-product-compliance
Lightning Source LLC
LaVergne TN
LVHW010421070526
838199LV00064B/5373